P9-DIG-093

DISCARD

The Totally
Secret Secret

For Colleen

Printed in Singapore

Reinforced binding

First Edition, May 2015

10 9 8 7 6 5 4 3 2 1

F850-6835-5-15015

Library of Congress Cataloging-in-Publication Data

Shea, Bob, author, illustrator.
Ballet Cat: the totally secret secret / by Bob Shea.—First edition.
pages cm
Summary: While Ballet Cat and Sparkles the Pony are trying to decide
what to play, they each share an important secret.
ISBN 978-1-4847-1378-5
[1. Best friends—Fiction. 2. Friendship—Fiction. 3. Play—Fiction.
4. Secrets—Fiction. 5. Cats—Fiction. 6. Ponies—Fiction.] I. Title.

PZ7.S53743Bal 2015
[E]—dc23   2014025070

www.DisneyBooks.com

BALLET CAT

The Totally Secret Secret

Bob Shea

Disney • HYPERION

Los Angeles   New York

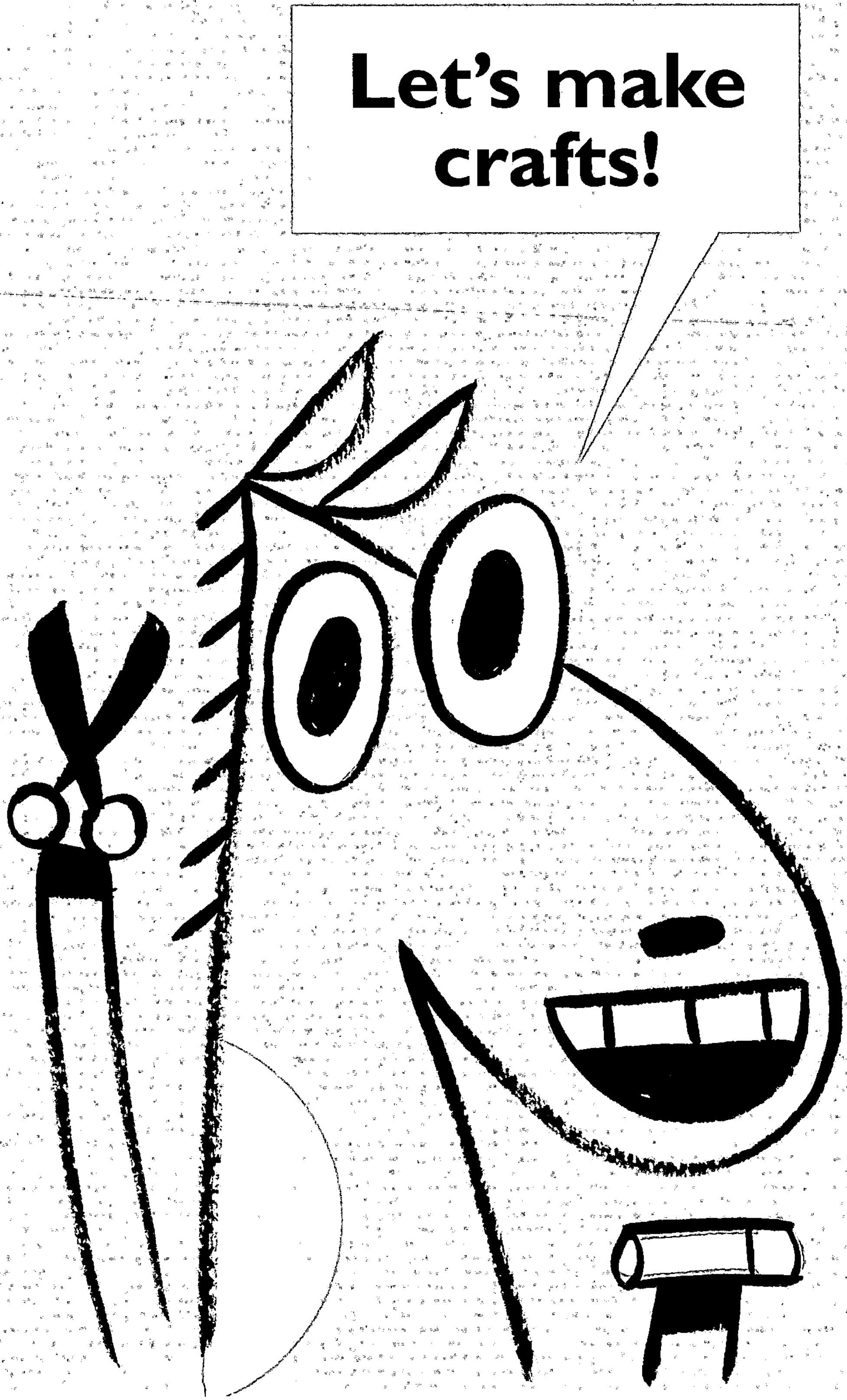
Let's make crafts!

Wait.
The lemonade will splash when we spin.

Now, let's see.
What goes well with leaping,
kicking, and spinning?
Think, cat, think!

We could play ballet.

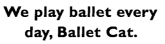

Is the secret that you are not so great at ballet? That is not a very *secret* secret, Sparkles.

No, it is not that.

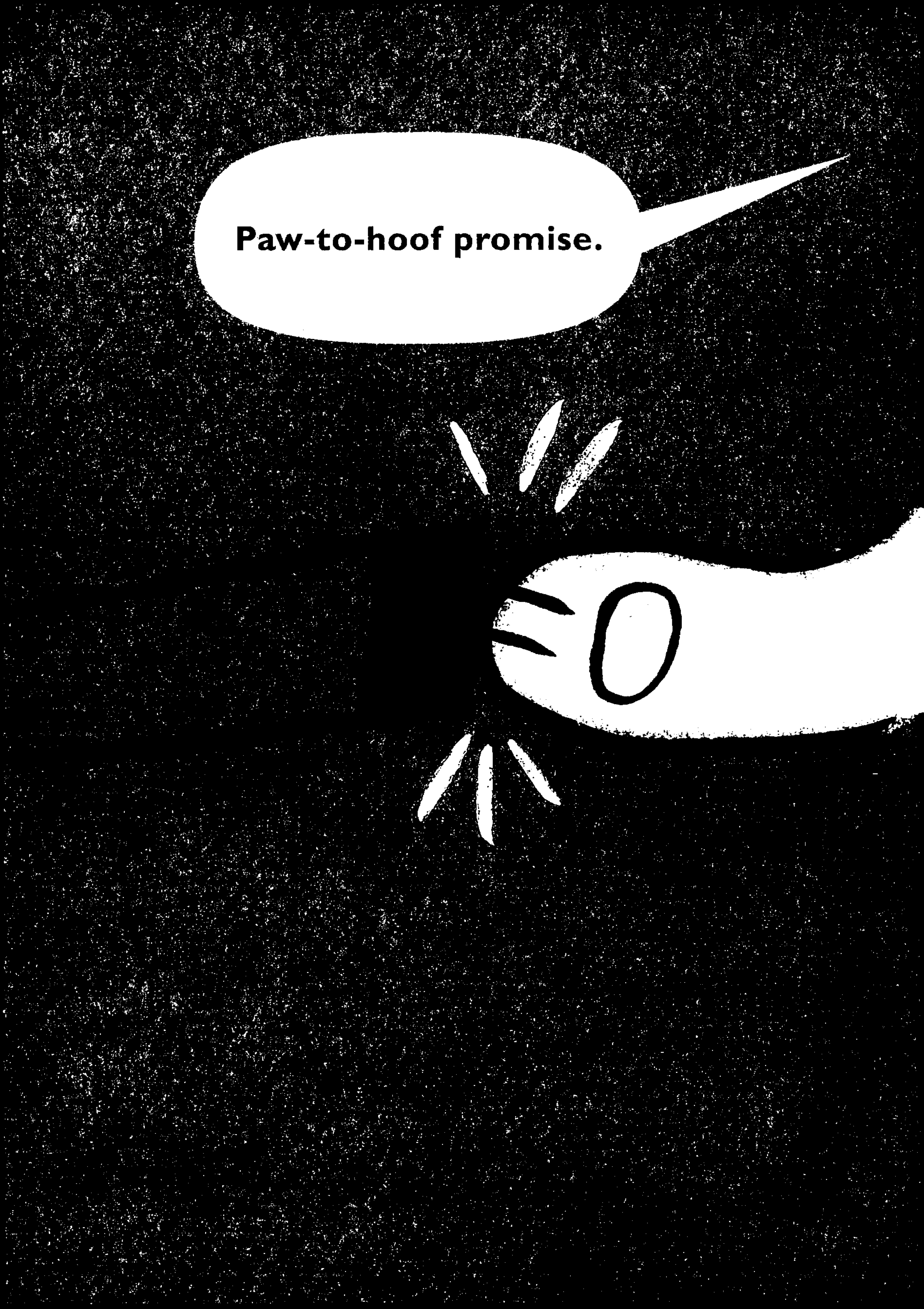
Paw-to-hoof promise.

Yes, I'm listening.

Sometimes
I don't want to
play ballet!

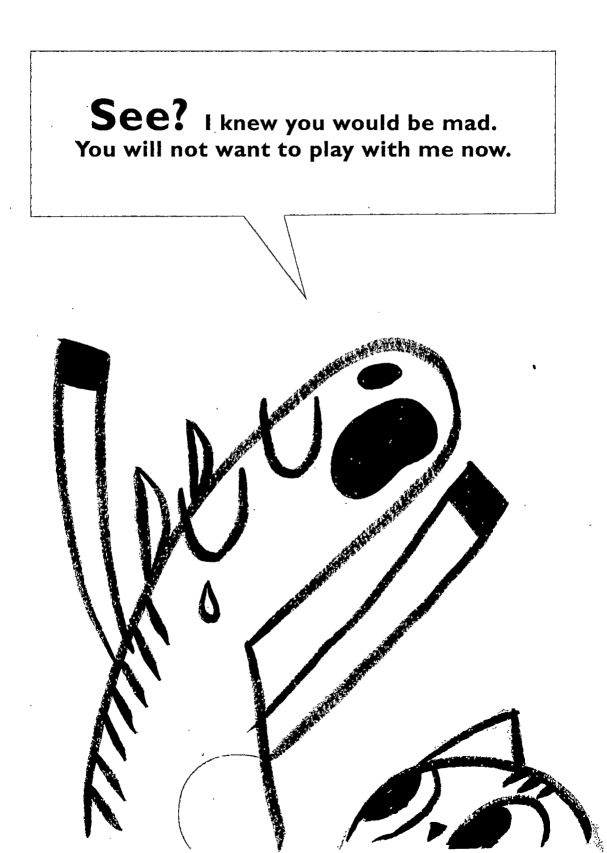

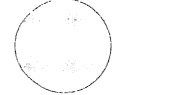